Karen's Haircut

Also in the Babysitters Little Sister series:

Look out for:

Karen's Haircut

Ann M. Martin

Illustrations by Susan Tang

Hippo Books
Scholastic Children's Books
London

Scholastic Children's Books,
Scholastic Publications Ltd,
7-9 Pratt Street, London NW1 0AE, UK

Scholastic Inc.,
730 Broadway, New York, NY 10003, USA

Scholastic Canada Ltd,
123 Newkirk Road, Richmond Hill,
Ontario, Canada L4C 3G5

Ashton Scholastic Pty Ltd,
P O Box 579, Gosford, New South Wales,
Australia

Ashton Scholastic Ltd,
Private Bag 1, Penrose, Auckland,
New Zealand

First published in the US by Scholastic Inc., 1990
First published in the UK by Scholastic Publications Ltd, 1992

Copyright © Ann M. Martin, 1990

BABYSITTERS LITTLE SISTER is a trademark of Scholastic Inc.

ISBN 0 590 55115 9

Typeset by A.J. Latham Ltd, Dunstable, Beds
Printed by Cox & Wyman Ltd, Reading, Berks

10 9 8 7 6 5 4 3 2 1

*This book
is in honour of the birth of
Maxwell Joseph Lieb*

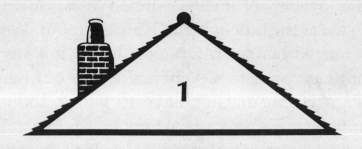

The Ugly Duckling

"Oh, I'm a lovely, lovely lady," I sang.

"Me too," said Nancy. "Would you like some tea?"

"Why, certainly. Lovely ladies must always have tea in the afternoon."

I'm Karen Brewer and I'm just seven. My friend Nancy Dawes is seven too. Nancy lives next door to my mother's house. She and I like to dress up and play lovely ladies. Nancy's got some good dressing-up clothes and so have I.

It was a Friday afternoon. I was at Nancy's

house and we'd been dressing up. We were the loveliest of lovely ladies. We sat down to tea at the little table in Nancy's room. We arranged her tea set. Nancy hasn't got any brothers or sisters. When she gets out her tea set, she doesn't have to worry about anyone messing it up. At my house I've got a little brother called Andrew. He's nearly five and sometimes he messes up my things.

At our tea party that day, Nancy was wearing blue high-heeled shoes, a long white petticoat, a straw hat, and nine necklaces. I was wearing red high heels, a long blue blouse, an apron, and a bride's veil.

"Yum, this tea is certainly delicious," I said.

"Scrumptious," added Nancy.

"Well, thank you very much for inviting me to tea, Miss Dawes. I'd better be going. I've got to do some shopping. I need nail varnish and hair curlers."

"May I come with you, Miss Brewer?"

asked Nancy. "I need nail varnish and hair curlers, too."

"Why, of course you may," I replied.

Nancy and I clumped through her house. Our high heels bumped along. We clumped into the living room.

"What lovely ladies!" exclaimed Nancy's mother.

We clumped into the kitchen. We clumped down the hall.

"I think the shop's in the bathroom," I said.

"Yes, I believe you are right," replied Lovely Lady Nancy.

So we clumped into the bathroom. I stopped in front of the long mirror. I looked up at myself carefully. I was dressed up, but my clothes couldn't hide my glasses. They couldn't hide my two front teeth either. Those teeth used to be smaller, then they fell out. When the grown-up teeth came, they were huge. They looked like rabbit teeth. Also, two of my side teeth on the top were loose. I hate those teeth, but when they come out, I hate the spaces they leave even more.

"I wish I were prettier," I said to Nancy.

"What's wrong with you?" she asked.

"Well, just look at me. I've got glasses, rabbit teeth, and loose teeth."

"I think you look fine," said Nancy.

But I didn't agree. I'm an ugly duckling, I thought.

Suddenly, lovely ladies didn't seem such a nice game. I didn't *feel* like a lovely lady. I was glad when Mummy arrived and said I had to come home. It was time for Andrew and me to go to Daddy's for the weekend.

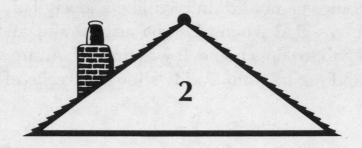

Little House, Big House

I live in two houses — Mummy's house and Daddy's house. Both of them are in Stoneybrook. Why do I live in two houses? Because Mummy and Daddy are divorced. This is what happened: a long time ago, Mummy and Daddy decided they didn't want to live together any more. After the divorce, they both got married again. Mummy married Seth and they live in a little house, which is the way they like things. Daddy married Elizabeth, who's got four children, and they live in a big, huge house – a mansion. Daddy's a millionaire.

Now Andrew and I live with Mummy and Seth most of the time, but every other weekend, and for two weeks in the summer, we live with Daddy and his big family.

As Andrew and I go to and fro so often between the little house and the big house, we've got two of almost everything – one at each house. We've got bicycles at each house. I've got a stuffed cat at each house, (one named Goosie, the other Moosie). I even ripped Tickly, my special blanket, in half so that I could have a piece at each house. With clothes and toys and other important things at each house, Andrew and I hardly have to pack at all when we go to Daddy's.

And do you know what? I've got a best friend at each house too. My little-house best friend is Nancy and my big-house best friend is Hannie Papadakis. She lives over the road from Daddy's house. Hannie and

Nancy and I are all in Miss Colman's second-grade class at Stoneybrook Academy.

Guess what I call Andrew and me? I call us two-two's. I'm Karen Two-Two and Andrew's Andrew Two-Two. That's because we've got two of everything — mummies, daddies, friends, houses, and more. I got the name from a book Miss Colman read to our class. It's called *Jacob Two-Two Meets the Hooded Fang*.

This is who lives in the little house apart from Andrew and me: Mummy, Seth (my stepfather), Rocky, Midgie, and Emily Junior. Rocky is Seth's cat and Midgie's his dog. Emily Junior's my rat. (You'll find out who she's named after in just a minute).

This is who lives in the big house apart from Andrew and me: first of all, Daddy and Elizabeth (my stepmother) and Elizabeth's children (my stepbrothers and stepsisters). They're Charlie and Sam, who are very grown-up and go to high school, David Michael, who's seven like me, and Kristy. I really love Kristy. She's one of my favourite people in the whole wide world. Kristy's thirteen and she babysits. She babysits for Andrew and me and lots of other children. She babysits so much that she and her friends started up a business called the Babysitters Club, and Kristy's the chairman.

Second, Emily Michelle and Nannie live in the big house. Emily Michelle is two years old. She's my adopted sister. Daddy and Elizabeth adopted her and she came from a far, faraway country called Vietnam. She's the one I named my rat after. Nannie's my step-grandmother. I love her a lot too. Nannie helps to look after Emily Michelle when everyone else is either at work or at school.

Oh, yes. Shannon and Boo-Boo live in the big house too. Shannon is David Michael's puppy and Boo-Boo's Daddy's fat old cat. I don't like him very much, and he doesn't like anyone except Daddy and Shannon. Boo-Boo scratches and bites and hisses.

Boo-Boo's the only bad thing about the big house, though. I love going to Daddy's.

I like being with all those people. The big house is usually exciting.

Maybe, I thought, I could forget about being an ugly duckling while I was at the big house.

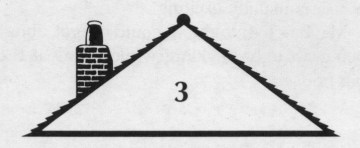

Professor

When Mummy drops Andrew and me off at the big house on Fridays, she usually calls, "See you later, alligators!"

Sometimes one of us answers, "In a while, crocodile!"

On this Friday, I yelled, "Not if I see you first!"

Mummy and Andrew and I laughed. Then Mummy waited in the car to see that we got inside Daddy's house safely. When the front door opened, I waved to Mummy. She drove away. Andrew and I would see her late on Sunday afternoon when she picked us up.

The person who'd opened the door was Kristy. Hurrah!

"Hello," said Kristy with a grin. She let Andrew and me in and closed the door behind us, then she gave us each a big hug.

Soon everyone in my big-house family had gathered in the hall. There were Daddy, Elizabeth, Nannie, Charlie, Sam, David Michael, Emily Michelle, and, of course, Kristy. Even Shannon came in. She pressed her wet nose into my hand. Boo-Boo didn't turn up, but I didn't care.

Everyone was hugging and kissing. Daddy lifted first me and then Andrew up into his arms. When he put me down, David Michael said cheerfully, "Hello, Professor!"

He calls me that because of my glasses. "Professor" isn't an unkind nickname, it's a nice one. David Michael's usually a pain in the neck, but sometimes he can be nice, and he was being nice when I first got

13

my glasses and he said he thought they made me look brainy, like a professor.

But that night I didn't want to look like a brainy professor. I wanted to look gorgeous. I wanted someone to say, "Hello, beautiful!" to me, only no one did.

I was feeling like an ugly duckling again, but I didn't tell anyone.

I really love evenings in the big house when everyone's at home. Those evenings are so busy and noisy. That night we ate dinner at the long table. We need an extra-long table because nine people have to sit at it. (Emily sits in a high chair.) Nannie had made chicken salad and sweetcorn for supper.

"You know what sweetcorn is, don't you, Andrew?" said Sam.

"A begetable," replied Andrew proudly.

"No. Corn is yellow teeth that have fallen out of old people's mouths."

"Ugh! How disgusting!" cried Andrew. "Nannie, why are you making us eat old teeth?"

14

"Sam's teasing you, darling," said Nannie gently. Then she gave Sam a look.

I tried to laugh, but I couldn't. Even though the tooth joke was funny, all I could think about was being an ugly duckling.

When we'd finished dinner, I helped Daddy and Elizabeth to clean up the kitchen. Then Andrew, David Michael, Emily Michelle, and I played hide-and-seek. I had to help Emily a lot because she doesn't understand the game. When it's her

15

turn to hide, she just sits and watches the rest of us.

We'd finished playing hide-and-seek when Hannie rang.

"Do you want to come to my house tomorrow?" she asked.

"Yes, please!" I replied. "Thanks."

Soon it was time to go to bed. I brushed my teeth with Andrew and David Michael and changed into my pyjamas. Kristy read me a bedtime story about a fairy princess.

I still felt like an ugly duckling.

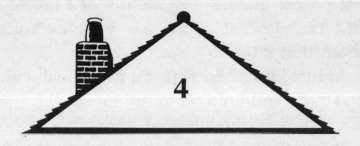

The Loose Tooth

On Saturday morning I woke up slowly. I like to lie in bed and think. I hugged Moosie and Tickly and wondered what Hannie and I would do at her house that day.

While I was wondering, I felt inside my mouth with my finger. There were those awful loose teeth. One of them was a lot looser than the other. I could push it quite far backwards and forwards. It was almost ready to come out. What if it came out while I was eating and I *swallowed* it? Ugh! Yuck! I had to get rid of that tooth.

I jumped out of bed, got dressed, and put on my glasses. I made my bed quickly and ran downstairs. I was very nervous about that tooth.

At breakfast, I tried to eat my cereal with one hand and hold on to the tooth with the other. It was difficult — and messy.

"Karen!" said Elizabeth when she noticed. "What are you doing?"

"Holding on to my tooth," I told her. "I don't want to swallow it."

"I don't think you need to worry about that," said Daddy.

I wasn't so sure.

When breakfast was over, Sam said to me, "Karen, I can get your tooth out in a jiffy. I know lots of ways."

"Do you?" I replied. Could I believe Sam? After all, he'd told Andrew that sweetcorn kernels were old teeth.

"Of course," replied Sam. "I can yank it out with pliers."

"NO!" I cried.

"Or *you* can hold on to the tooth, and I'll

pull your hand out of your mouth."

"NO!"

"All right. There's only one way left. I'll tie a string round your tooth. Very carefully," he added. "And I'll tie the other end of the string to a doorknob. Then I'll slam the door shut and bam! Your tooth will come out. It'll fly through the air on the string."

Well, that sounded rather interesting. I'd never seen one of my teeth fly through the air on a string.

"All right," I told Sam. "You can tie my tooth up."

Sam got some string and a pair of scissors. Then we went to my room. I sat on my bed. It took a while, but at last Sam managed to tie the string round my loose tooth. Then he unrolled a long piece of string and cut it off. He tied the other end to the doorknob.

"Now you stay there," said Sam, "while I slam the door."

"Is this going to hurt?" I asked.

"Maybe just for a second."

19

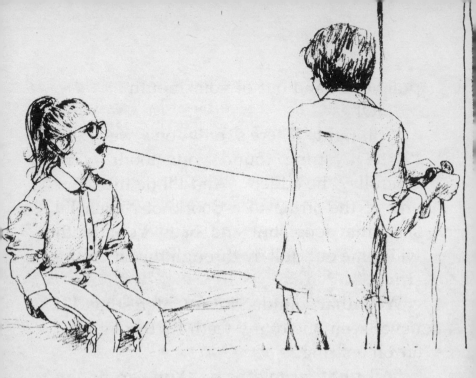

Sam put his hand on the door. "Okay," he said. "One . . . two . . ."

"STOP!" I cried. "Forget it. I don't want you to slam the door."

Sam took his hand away. "Are you sure?" he asked.

I nodded.

"All right." Sam untied my tooth. "Cluck, cluck, cluck, cluck . . . CHICKEN!" he cried.

I didn't care. I told Daddy about my tooth. And do you know what? Daddy got a tissue and pulled it out — just like that! It didn't hurt a bit, but it did bleed a little. Elizabeth helped me rinse out my mouth with salty water.

I looked at myself in the bathroom mirror. Yuck! Now I had glasses, rabbit teeth, one loose tooth, and a gap in my mouth where the other tooth had been.

Ugly duckling, ugly duckling, I thought.

But at least I could leave my tooth under my pillow for the Tooth Fairy that night.

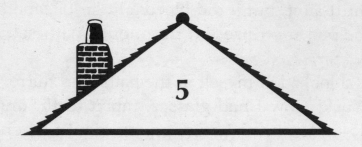

The Other Loose Tooth

It was time to go to Hannie's house. I crossed the road carefully, ran across the Papadakises' front lawn, and rang their doorbell. Hannie answered it.

"Hello," I said. "Notice anything different about me?" I grinned broadly.

"Oh!" cried Hannie. "Your tooth's come out at last." She let me in.

"Yes," I said. "And look how loose *this* one is." I wiggled the other tooth backwards and forwards with my tongue.

"Ugh!" said Hannie. "How disgusting!"

I smiled. I was teasing Hannie. She doesn't like loose teeth any more than I do.

"Well," said Hannie, "what do you want to do today?"

"Let's play It!" I suggested. "We could get Andrew, David Michael, and Linny to play with us." (Linny's Hannie's older brother. He and David Michael are friends.)

"Okay," said Hannie.

So we found the boys, and then we began running around Hannie's garden. Andrew was It first. He took ages to catch someone. That's probably because his legs are shorter than anyone else's.

At last he caught Hannie. Then Hannie was It and she caught me. At last *I* was It. I love being It.

I ran all over Hannie's garden. First I chased Linny. I almost caught him, but suddenly I changed direction. I turned round and ran after Hannie. Then I changed direction again. This was to confuse everybody. When they were really mixed up, I chased David Michael. As he was sure that I'd change direction, he wasn't running very fast. But when he saw that I really *was* after him, he ran faster. I ran faster, too. I was running as fast as I'd ever run. I stretched out my hand. "You're . . . *It!*" I cried. I stretched my arm out so far to touch him that I lost my balance and fell down.

"Oof!" I said. Then, "Oh! Oh, no!" I'd fallen on my mouth, and — yes, my tooth had come out. My other loose tooth was rattling around in my mouth. I don't think it had been ready to come out, but it was out anyway.

"What's wrong?" cried Hannie. She ran over to me. The boys crowded round too.

"I've lost the other tooth," I said. I spat it into my hand. My mouth was bleeding again.

"Ugh!" said Linny. "How disgusting."

But Hannie said, "Come inside. Mummy will see to your mouth."

So Hannie and I went into the Papadakises' kitchen, and Mrs Papadakis dabbed the gap

24

in my mouth with a tissue. Then she gave me a glass of salty water — just like Elizabeth had done — and I rinsed till there was no more blood.

"Hey!" said Hannie. "Tonight you'll have to put *two* teeth under your pillow for the Tooth Fairy. I wonder if you get anything special for losing two teeth in one day."

"Maybe," I said. I wanted to go home. I'd just peeped at myself in the bathroom mirror

and I looked . . . like a freak. I had rabbit teeth, and gaps in my mouth everywhere, and my awful old glasses. I was the ugliest duckling of all.

But I didn't want to be a baby, so when Hannie said, "Let's play It again. The boys are still here," I said, "All right."

It was the last thing I wanted to do.

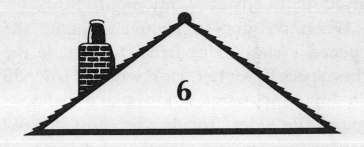

Hannie's Wedding

The boys were still at the Papadakises' but they were tired of It. They were in the front drive, pretending they were space invaders.

"Grrrr! I am an alien," said Andrew to Hannie and me. "I'll eat you up."

"And I'll blast you with my ray gun," said Linny, pointing a stick at us.

I looked at Hannie. She looked at me.

"Let's go to my room and play," she said. (Hannie's collection of dressing-up clothes is almost as good as Nancy's and mine.)

"Yes," I said. I don't like playing space invaders. In any case, my mouth hurt.

When we got to Hannie's room, she opened a chest. Her father had made the chest specially for her. He'd written HANNIE on top, and painted bears and balloons round the sides. Inside the chest are old hats and shoes and gloves and dresses, as well as a cowgirl suit, a ballerina's tutu, and a policeman's uniform.

"Shall we be lovely ladies?" asked Hannie in a lovely-lady voice.

"But of course," I replied.

We put on dresses. We put on hats. We put on scarves and gloves and jewellery. Then we walked out of Hannie's room. We looked at ourselves in the long mirror in her parents' bedroom.

"Yuk!" I said.

I turned round and marched back to Hannie's room, took off my lovely-lady clothes and put them back in her chest.

Hannie watched me. "What's wrong?" she asked.

"I'm not a lovely lady," I told her.

"Neither am I," said Hannie. "We're just pretending."

"No, I mean I'm not pretty. I'm not even sweet. I'm an ugly duckling."

Hannie frowned.

"*Look* at me," I said. I pointed out all the ugly things.

"Hmm," said Hannie. "Perhaps you'd feel better if you got your hair cut or something. Maybe you need a change."

"I asked Mummy and Daddy if I could have contact lenses instead of glasses, and they both said, 'No. Not till you're fourteen.'"

"*Fourteen!*" cried Hannie. "You won't be fourteen for years."

"I know."

"Well, what about a new haircut? I like your hair the way it is now, but wouldn't it be exciting to go to a beauty salon and get a haircut? Something new and special and different?"

"Yes!" I exclaimed. Beauty salons are great. Once I went on an ocean cruise on a huge ship. On the ship were swimming pools and restaurants and even a beauty salon. And I went to the beauty salon *by myself* and had a manicure.

"Perhaps," I said excitedly to Hannie, "I could have my nails done, too. I'd like them painted pink."

"Well, there's a new beauty salon in town," Hannie told me. "It's called Gloriana's House of Hair. Maybe you could go there."

30

"Yes!" I cried. "I'll ask Daddy about it when I get home."

"Do you know what?" said Hannie. "This is perfect, because Scott and I are getting married soon. After your beauty treatment you'll look lovely. Then you can be the bridesmaid at our wedding." (Hannie's in love with Scott Hsu, a new boy who's moved into our road. He doesn't go to our school.)

"Thanks," I said, "but I thought you wanted me to be the photographer at your wedding."

"I did. But I want you to be a beautiful bridesmaid even more."

"Can you wait till after my beauty treatment?" I asked.

"Of course," replied Hannie. "The wedding date hasn't been arranged yet."

"Goody! I can't wait!" I exclaimed.

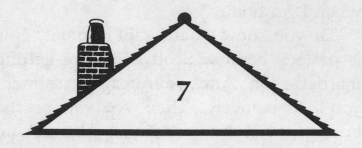

Waiting for Tuesday

I left Hannie's that afternoon after lunch. Hannie's father had made fruit salad for us. Yum! Strawberries are my favourite. Do you know what Andrew calls them? He calls them "strawbabies"!

When it was time for me to go home, Mrs Papadakis gave me a little white box. "Your tooth's in here," she told me.

"Thank you," I replied.

I ran to my house.

"Look, everybody!" I cried. "I lost my other tooth at Hannie's! Here it is! Now I can put *two* teeth under my pillow for the Tooth Fairy."

My family *was* impressed.

"What do you think happens if you lose two teeth in one day?" I asked them.

"I think," replied Sam, "that the Tooth Fairy says to herself, 'Hmm. Karen *is* lucky to have lost two teeth at once. I don't think she needs a surprise under her pillow. She's already had enough excitement.' "

"Sa-*am!*" I cried.

Later on, I found Daddy outside, weeding the herb garden. No one else was in the garden so it was a good time to ask him about getting some beauty treatment at Gloriana's House of Hair.

"Daddy?" I said. I sat down at the edge of the garden.

"Yes?" Daddy was hoeing. He stopped, leaned on the hoe, and looked at me.

"Daddy, I feel like an ugly duckling. My teeth are awful. I've got big rabbit teeth in front, and the gaps where my other teeth fell out, and I've got to wear glasses. Could

I please, please, *please* get my hair cut? At Gloriana's House of Hair? It's a new place in town."

"I don't know," Daddy replied. "A posh beauty salon?"

"*Please?* I know I'll feel better with a new haircut . . . and a manicure . . . and a pedicure. Pink toenails would look lovely."

"I think a haircut and a manicure will be enough," said Daddy. "But I'll have to talk to Mummy first. She has to agree to this."

"All right. Thank you!" I cried.

So Daddy and Mummy talked on the phone. Mummy said I could get my hair cut and have a manicure. Yippee! Daddy said he would pay for my beauty treatment. He even made the appointment for me. I would get my hair cut on Tuesday after school.

That night, I put my teeth under my pillow. Guess what was there when I woke up on Sunday? A new hair slide! Now, how did the Tooth Fairy know I wanted a pretty new blue hairslide? I suppose it's because she's magic.

I liked my hairslide a lot, but I didn't like waiting for Tuesday afternoon. That was very hard. Hannie and Nancy both helped make the wait a little easier, though.

On Monday, Nancy said, "Karen, if you want a good haircut, you should find a picture of the style you want and take it to the beauty salon with you."

"Oh. That's a good idea," I replied.

"Thank you." So Nancy and I looked through some magazines till I found a haircut I liked.

"Here! This is it," I said. I cut the picture out of the magazine.

Hannie helped make the wait easier by phoning me about her wedding. She rang seven times. She kept asking things like, "Do you think I should wear flowers in my hair?" And, "Who should we invite to the wedding?" And, "Do you think your haircut will look good, Karen? I want you to be the most beautiful bridesmaid ever. You'll look pretty, won't you?"

"I hope so," I answered. I really did hope so!

Karen's Beauty Treatment

At long last Tuesday arrived. Mummy picked me up after school. Andrew was with her.

Bother! I didn't want my little brother at Gloriana's House of Hair. He'd probably damage something. And I wanted to look like a grown-up person who didn't have a four-year-old brother. I hoped Andrew would sit quietly and behave himself.

Mummy drove into the town centre. She parked in front of a really smart building. It was mostly glass with a silver door. Bright pink neon lights spelled out Gloriana's House of Hair like this:

Gloriana's House of Hair

"Ooh!" I said. "Isn't it beautiful? I bet Gloriana's beautiful too. She's got the most beautiful name I've ever heard. Andrew, you'll have to behave yourself. Gloriana's is one of those places where you mustn't touch anything."

"Don't you worry about Andrew," said Mummy. "I'll watch him. If he gets fidgety, we'll go for a walk. You won't mind staying in the beauty salon alone for a few minutes, will you?"

"Oh, no!" I said. (I'd feel much more grown-up if that happened.)

Mummy and Andrew and I went into Gloriana's House of Hair. There were mirrors and pink neon decorations everywhere!

The woman behind the desk said, "Let's see. Karen Brewer. You're here for a haircut and a manicure, is that right?"

I nodded.

"Okay. Sally's going to give you the manicure first."

Sally? Bother! I wanted Gloriana to do everything.

"And then," the woman went on, "Gloriana will cut your hair."

Goody!

Mummy and Andrew sat in the waiting area, looking at magazines.

I followed Sally to her manicure chair. I chose bright pink polish.

When Sally had finished my nails, she led me to a chair in front of a basin. "Keep your hands very still," she told me. "Your nails aren't dry yet."

"All right," I replied. While my nails dried, a man washed my hair. Then a woman wrapped a towel round my head.

"I'm Gloriana," she said. "Are you ready for your haircut?"

"Yes," I replied. "I've even got a picture of what I want." I gave it to Gloriana.

I watched Gloriana while she looked at the picture. I decided I didn't like Gloriana's hair at all. Some of it was short, some was long, some was dark, and some was light. But I supposed it didn't matter what Gloriana's hair looked like, as long as she copied the picture and gave me the haircut I wanted.

I sat down in the haircutting chair. I was

so excited, I could feel butterflies in my tummy. Gloriana began to snip away.

The cut I wanted was a nice simple one. I wanted shoulder-length hair (so I could still wear hairslides and ribbons in it) with a fringe in front.

Gloriana had been cutting my hair for a while when Mummy came over to me and said, "Andrew's getting fidgety. I'm going to take him for a walk. We'll be back in ten minutes, okay?"

"Okay," I answered.

While Mummy and Andrew were gone, Gloriana kept cutting away. She snipped and cut and cut and snipped. My long hair fell in a pile on the floor.

Suddenly I realized something awful. My hair was getting *too* short, but I was afraid to tell Gloriana! I wanted Mummy.

By the time Mummy and Andrew came back, Gloriana had finished doing my hair. It wasn't the cut I'd asked for. I was practically bald.

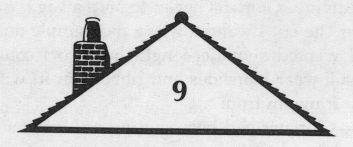

The Bride of Frankenstein

Well, all right, I wasn't practically bald, but my hair was much shorter than I'd wanted. I had a fringe in front, but the rest of my hair was cut close to my head, except for some long hair in the back that came down to my shoulders. It looked really weird. Most of my hair was too short for hairslides and ribbons.

When Mummy got back, she looked surprised. "Karen!" she exclaimed. "Is that what you asked for?" She looked suspiciously at Gloriana.

"*No,*" I replied. My lips were quivering.

"It's the latest cut," Gloriana told us. "Karen's very fashionable now."

I didn't care what Gloriana said. I *hated* my hair.

I cried all the way home. (Mummy said my hair would grow back.)

My nails looked lovely, but with my glasses, my rabbit teeth, my missing teeth, and my horrible, awful hair, I looked worse than ever.

When I woke up the next morning, my tummy felt funny. I knew I had butterflies again, only these weren't excited butterflies. They were scared butterflies.

How could I face the other children at school? They were all going to tease me, I just knew it. Especially Ricky Torres. Yicky Ricky Torres. He would tease me the worst of all. He would probably call me a horrible name. I was right.

I tried to get to Miss Colman's room late. I hoped I could slide into my seat just in time for the Register. But I wasn't late enough. Miss Colman hadn't even arrived yet. And when I came in, everyone just stared at me, even Hannie and Nancy.

Then Yicky Ricky said, "Look! Here comes the Bride of Frankenstein!"

He meant me.

All the boys and a couple of girls started calling me the Bride of Frankenstein. But that wasn't the worst thing. The worst

thing happened when I ran to the back of the room to be with Hannie and Nancy. (We used to sit together, but after I got my glasses, Miss Colman moved me to the front row.)

I wanted my friends to make me feel better. Nancy tried. She said, "Karen, your hair's quite . . . interesting."

But *Hannie* said, "What happened?"

"Gloriana didn't copy the picture I gave her," I replied sadly.

Hannie looked thoughtful. Then she said, "I − you − I − Karen, I don't know how to tell you this, but you can't be my bridesmaid. Not while you look like that."

I almost began to cry, but Miss Colman came into the room then. Everyone sat down. The day began. It was a horrible, long day. I couldn't concentrate on my work at all. And in the corridor on the way to lunch, two fifth-grade girls pointed at me. That was when I knew for certain that I looked like the Bride of Frankenstein. Fifth-graders never take any notice of second-graders. Not unless something about them is wrong or funny.

I was most upset about Hannie, though. How could she be so unkind to me? She was supposed to be one of my best friends.

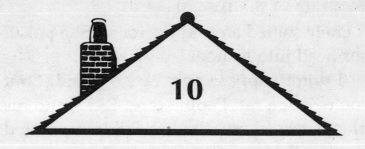

10

Tiffanie

After school that day, Mummy picked Nancy and me up and drove us home.

As Nancy ran up her front drive, she called, " 'Bye, Karen! See you tomorrow!"

I didn't answer her.

"Karen?" said Mummy. "What's wrong? You didn't say a word in the car. Do you feel all right?"

I didn't answer Mummy either.

I marched up to my room, closed my door and took Emily Junior out of her cage.

"Emily, Emily, Emily," I said. "Look at

me. Do you care if I'm an ugly duckling or the Bride of Frankenstein?"

Emily sniffed around my room. She poked her head into a shoe.

"I don't suppose you care," I said. "But you're just a rat. People care. Ricky and his friends teased me, the big children pointed at me, and one of my best friends in the world isn't my best friend any more. She won't let me be in her wedding, just because of my hair. I'm glad you're a rat. Rats are nicer than people."

Sniff, sniff, sniff went Emily Junior. I put her back in her cage.

Then I picked up Goosie, my stuffed cat. I sat on my bed and leaned against the wall. I made Goosie stare at me.

"Well?" I said. "Do *you* think I look like the Bride of Frankenstein?"

I made Goosie nod his head.

"Thanks a lot," I told him.

Then I held him up to my ear. "What? What did you say? . . . That if I can't look beautiful, at least I can have a beautiful name? Gosh, that's a good idea, Goosie. Thanks!"

I put Goosie down and thought of beautiful names. Yesterday I'd thought Gloriana was a beautiful name, but not today. Not after what Gloriana had done to me. Hmm. Katie? No. Sarah? No. Those were pretty names, but I wanted a *beautiful* name like . . . like Tiffanie! That was a gorgeous name!

At dinner that night I said, "Listen, everybody — I've got a new name —"

"How can you have a new name?" interrupted Andrew.

"I just have," I told him. "It's Tiffanie. Isn't that beautiful?"

"It's lovely," said Seth. "Why do you need a new name?"

"I need to pretend I'm beautiful," I replied. "So please remember to call me Tiffanie."

"All right," agreed Mummy and Seth and Andrew.

But later, Seth said, "Have you finished your supper, Karen?"

And Andrew said, "Will you play with me, Karen?"

I had to remind both of them that I was Tiffanie.

When I'd finished my homework that evening, I stood in front of the mirror. I looked at myself from my head to my feet and back again.

I decided I needed more sparkle. Maybe my new haircut was ugly, and maybe my glasses and teeth were ugly, but I could still try to look glamorous.

So I painted over my pink nail varnish

and put on sparkly gold varnish. A friend of Kristy's had given it to me.

There. Now I had a beautiful name and *very* beautiful nails. I was becoming glamorous.

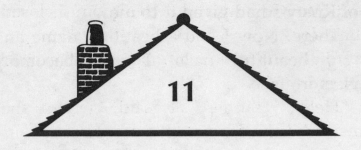

"No Way!"

It was time to make a phone call.

I thought I knew just how to get my former best friend back.

"Mummy?" I asked.

Mummy was in the living room reading to Andrew. She was reading *Let's Be Enemies*, which Andrew likes a lot.

"Yes?" replied Mummy.

"May I make a phone call? I need to use the phone in your room so that the call will be private."

"Okay," said Mummy.

"Thank you!" I cried. I dashed upstairs and into Mummy and Seth's room. I closed their door.

I dialled Hannie's number. I was excited about my idea.

"Hello, Hannie," I said, when she answered the phone. "It's me, Karen."

"Oh . . . hello," said Hannie.

"Hannie, I've got something to tell you. I'm much more beautiful now than I was at school today. I'm glamorous. I've got a new

name — Tiffanie — and I've painted my nails sparkly gold. They're the most elegant nails in Stoneybrook. So can I be your bridesmaid after all?"

"What did you say your name is?" asked Hannie.

"Tiffanie," I answered. "Um, Tiffanie Titania Brewer."

"And *what* colour are your nails?"

"Sparkly gold."

"But your hair and your teeth are still the same?" asked Hannie.

"Yes," I admitted.

"Then you can't be in my wedding," Hannie told me. "Definitely not! I only want a beautiful, *perfect* bridesmaid at my wedding. You're not perfect."

"Oh." I felt like a broken biscuit — the one in the packet no one will eat until all the whole ones have been eaten. I couldn't think of anything to say to Hannie except, "Goodbye."

"Goodbye," replied Hannie.

We hung up.

I almost cried. That was how sad I felt. But then I felt something else, too. I was ANGRY! What Hannie was doing wasn't fair.

After I got into bed that night, I lay awake for a long time and made plans. I wasn't sure how to be perfect, but I had some ideas about how to be more glamorous.

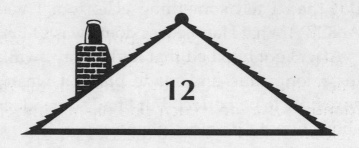

The New Karen

As soon as I woke up the next morning, I hopped out of bed. The first thing I did was check my nails. They looked *perfect*. They were sparkly and gold and I hadn't chipped a single one.

Then I looked in the mirror. Yuck! There were my awful teeth and my awful hair. I tried brushing my hair several different ways. That didn't help. My hair looked as awful as ever.

But I said to myself in the mirror, "You are Tiffanie. Tiffanie Titania Brewer. That is a beautiful name. And you can be very glamorous."

I got dressed. Then I put on five pink plastic bracelets and eight rings, one on each finger. I get the rings from the dentist's surgery. Each one has a different coloured stone. When the rings were on, I put on five necklaces. Then I slipped a stretchy blue beaded bracelet over my foot. Nobody in my class had ever worn an ankle bracelet. I would be the first. I was really going to surprise the other children at school!

When Seth dropped me off at school that day, I felt nervous. What would everyone think of the New Karen? I tried to walk into my classroom with confidence. I tried to walk in as if I dressed like this every day.

I sat down at my desk. I could tell that all the other children were staring at me. I could *feel* their eyes. But no one said a word. That was probably because Yicky Ricky wasn't there yet.

After I had put my things away in my

desk, I walked to the back of the room. A crowd of girls were standing there.

"Hello," I said.

"Hello," they replied. Well, everyone said hello except Hannie. She wasn't talking to me.

"Guess what? I've got a new name," I told the other girls.

Hannie rolled her eyes, but Nancy said, "What is it?"

"It's Tiffanie Titania Brewer."

"Ooh, that's beautiful!" said Natalie Springer.

But a few moments later, Nancy said, "Hey, Karen, look what I —"

"My name's *Tiffanie*," I interrupted her.

Just then Ricky came into our classroom. Uh-oh.

"Look, there's the Bride of Frankenstein!" was the first thing Ricky said.

"For your information, Richard, my name is Tiffanie. And by the way, your glasses make you look like an owl," I said loudly.

Everybody laughed. The boys started

hooting at Ricky. "Who-who-who! Who-who-who!"

Ricky sat down, looking cross, but he didn't bother me all morning. I think he was afraid I'd call him another name. In fact, Ricky was the only one in the class who remembered *not* to call me Karen.

Natalie said, "I like your nails, Karen."

Jannie Gilbert said, "Sit with me at lunch, Karen."

Nancy said, "I've got a new dress, Karen. Come to my house after school and see it."

"Okay," I replied.

But Ricky said, "You look very, um, pretty, T-Taffy."

"Thank you," I replied, even though he'd got the name wrong. At least he'd tried.

Hannie didn't call me Tiffanie or Taffy or Karen or anything. She still wasn't speaking to me. I suppose it was because I wasn't perfect . . . yet.

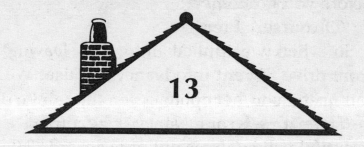

Krystal

When school was over, Mrs Dawes, Nancy's mother, picked Nancy and me up and drove us home.

On the way, I said, "Guess what, Mrs Dawes? I've got a new name. It's Tiffanie Titania Brewer. Do you like it?"

"It's . . . very nice," replied Mrs Dawes.

I saw her glance in the rearview mirror at Nancy and me.

"Hey, Karen —" Nancy began.

"Tiffanie, Tiffanie, TIFFANIE!" I cried.

"Sorry," said Nancy. "Hey, Tiffanie, can

you come in and look at my new dress before you go home?"

"Of course," I replied.

So when we pulled into the Dawes' front drive, I went into Nancy's house. We ran upstairs to her room.

"Here it is," said Nancy. She pulled a beautiful yellow dress out of her wardrobe. "It's for my cousin's bar mitzvah. But first I'm wearing it to the wedding."

"What wedding?" I asked.

"Hannie's."

"*Hannie's?!*"

"Hasn't she invited you?" asked Nancy.

"No," I replied crossly. "She's angry with me and I'm angry with her. Well, I'd better go. Mummy doesn't know I'm at your house. I'll phone you tonight, okay?"

"Okay," replied Nancy. She looked worried. " 'Bye, Karen."

" 'Bye!" I called. I didn't even bother to remind her that my name was Tiffanie.

" 'Bye, Karen," said Mrs Dawes as I ran through the front door.

" 'Bye, Mrs Dawes."

All right, maybe Tiffanie was a hard name to remember. Maybe it was too different from Karen. By the time I'd reached my own house next door, I'd decided something. I needed another new and glamorous name, but I needed one that started with the same sound as *Karen*.

All afternoon I thought of names: Camille, Carlotta, Caroline, Catherine, Candace, Clarissa, Cornelia, Kimberly, Kerry, Kelly.

By dinnertime, I had another new name for myself — Krystal. Usually, you spell that name with a C: Crystal. But I would spell it with a K to make it more like Karen.

I told my little-house family my new name. Seth remembered to call me Krystal! Mummy forgot and called me Karen, and Andrew finally called me Tiffanie.

I wasn't going to give up, though. I phoned Nancy that night. "I've got another new name," I told her. "It's much easier to remember. My new name's Krystal."

"Krystal," repeated Nancy. Then she said, "Kar — I mean, um, oh well, what's the matter with you and Hannie?"

"We're having a quarrel," I answered. "Hannie says I'm not perfect so I can't be in her wedding. I was going to be her bridesmaid."

"That's not fair!" exclaimed Nancy.

"Are you going to be angry with Hannie now?" I asked hopefully.

"No," replied Nancy. "I can't be. She hasn't done anything to me. I'm still

Hannie's friend, and I'm still your friend, too."

"Okay. Thanks, Nancy. I mean, thank you for being my friend even though I've got ugly hair and ugly teeth."

"That's all right."

"Goodnight, Nancy."

"Goodnight . . . Kristy?"

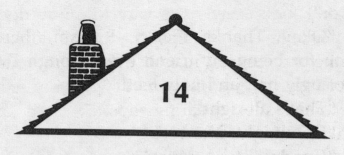

Gazelle, Desiree, and Chantal

The next day, Friday, I went to school as Krystal Karlotta Brewer.

I wore my sparkly gold nail polish and all my jewellery. And I put something secret in my skirt pocket before I left our house. As soon as Seth dropped me off at school, I ran to the girls' cloakroom. I put my school bag and my lunch box on the floor. Then I pulled the something out of my pocket.

It was a tube of red lipstick. Mummy had thrown it away while there was still some perfectly good lipstick at the end of the tube.

I smeared the lipstick all over my mouth. I didn't look exactly the way Mummy does when she wears lipstick, but I looked quite interesting, maybe even glamorous. One thing was certain: I was the only second-grader wearing lipstick, and an ankle bracelet.

I marched proudly into my classroom.

Everyone noticed the lipstick straight away.

"You're wearing make-up!" cried Nancy.

"Lipstick!" exclaimed Natalie Springer. "Wow!"

(Hannie looked at me, but she didn't say anything.)

"Karen — " began Jannie Gilbert.

"Excuse me," I said, "but I've got another name. This one's easier to remember. Now, I'm Krystal Karlotta Brewer."

"Christina?" said Natalie.

"No, *Krystal*."

Nobody could remember Krystal, either (except for Ricky Torres). I gave the other children in my class a whole week to remember it, too. During that time, I found some blusher that Mummy had thrown away and I started secretly wearing that with the lipstick. My friends were impressed. They thought I was glamorous. Hannie even spoke to me. She said, "You still can't be in my wedding, *Karen*."

After a week I decided I needed another new name. Krystal wasn't working. So on Monday I told my friends that I was Gazelle. Ricky remembered. He said, "Here's your pencil, Gazelle," when I dropped it on the floor. But Nancy called me Gardenia and the boys (except for Ricky) called me Godzilla.

I quickly changed my name to Desirée. Ricky called me Desirée, Natalie called me Dee-Dee, and Nancy, looking confused, called me Dezimay (or something like that). Hannie called me Karen and said I still couldn't be in her wedding.

That was Wednesday. On Friday, I changed my name to Chantal. I added hair ribbons to my outfit. When I wore just one, it looked funny with my short hair. But when I put on six at the same time, I looked more

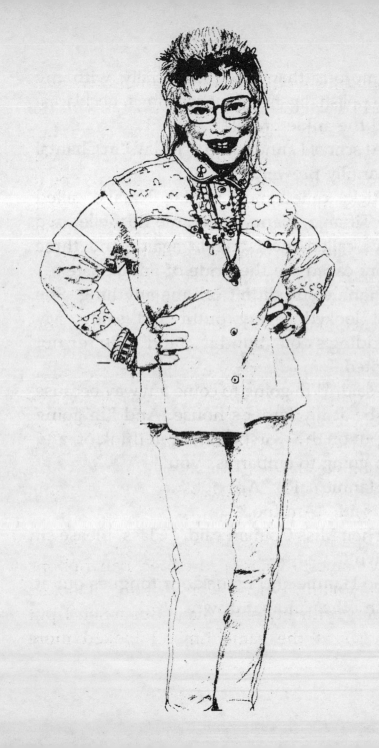

glamorous than ever, especially with my nail polish, lipstick, blusher, rings, necklaces, and the ankle bracelet.

At school I announced, "Today I'm Chantal Chantilly Brewer."

Ricky called me Chantal, Natalie called me Tiffanie, Nancy called me Rochelle, two boys called me Godzilla again, and three more called me the Bride of Frankenstein.

Hannie still didn't call me anything. She just looked at my outfit and said, "My wedding's on Sunday, and you're not invited."

I said, "I'm going to come anyway because I'll be at my father's house. And I'm going to put on the worst outfit I can think of, and I'm going to embarrass you."

Hannie said, "Are not."

I said, "Am too."

Then Miss Colman said, "Class, please sit down."

So Hannie and I stuck our tongues out at each other and sat down.

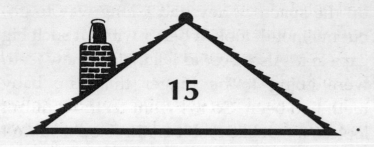

15

The Big Children

It was that Friday, the day I changed my name to Chantal, that I noticed something. That morning I had looked at myself in the bathroom mirror for a long time, and guess what? My hair was growing! It was still short, but it looked an awful lot better than it had after Gloriana had first cut it. That was why I'd decided to wear the six hair ribbons. My haircut, I decided, wasn't so bad, no matter what Hannie said.

Guess what else? My teeth looked better,

too. New ones were growing in and filling up the spaces. They had a long way to go, but my mouth looked better without such big gaps in it. Also, I could tell that the new teeth were going to be bigger than the baby teeth had been. So my front teeth wouldn't look so much like rabbit teeth. They wouldn't stand out as much.

I smiled at myself in the mirror. That made me look even better. I remembered a song from the play *Annie*, and I sang part of it to Goosie when I went back to my bedroom.

"You're never fully dressed without a smile," I sang.

Goosie just stared at me. It's such a shame to have buttons for eyes.

Then Mummy called me. She reminded me that after school, Andrew and I would be going to Daddy's for the weekend.

She didn't remember to call me Chantal.

I didn't mind. I was feeling too good on Friday. I also didn't mind very much either when Hannie and I stuck our tongues out at each other again. Then something really exciting happened. It was almost the end of the school day. I had been to the girls' cloakroom, and I was walking back to Miss Colman's class, when I saw two big children — fifth-grade girls. They were walking towards me. They tried to point at me without my seeing, but I saw anyway.

Uh-oh, I thought. They're going to tease me. But they didn't. As we passed each other, they smiled at me. I smiled back.

When the bell rang at the end of the day, I told Nancy what had happened. "You know what?" I said. "I think they liked my hair."

"*Really?*" replied Nancy. I could tell she was impressed. Big children had liked something about a second-grader!

But Hannie said, "Of course they liked your hair. Of course they did." I could tell she didn't believe me.

I didn't care what Hannie said. I'd seen

the big children smile at me. I thought they liked my hair. So I felt pretty. (Well, almost pretty.)

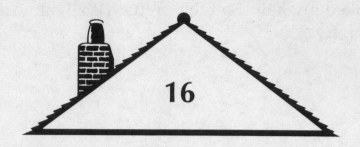

Hannie's Accident

On Saturday morning I woke up in my room in the big house.

"Good morning, Moosie. Good morning, Tickly," I said.

I lay in bed and wondered what I would do that day. Usually I play with Hannie. But I knew she wouldn't phone me. And I certainly wouldn't phone her.

At breakfast I announced, "I'm bored."

All my big-house family was at the kitchen table. I was hoping Kristy would invite me to go shopping with her and her friend

Mary Anne. Or that Daddy would say, "Come and help me in the garden."

Instead, Elizabeth said, "Why don't you take Emily outside to play. I think she'd like that."

Before I could answer her, Andrew said, "Let's teach her to play It. She doesn't know how. I bet she'd like running after us."

"Well . . . all right," I said, even though I thought Emily was too little to understand It. I didn't want to disappoint Andrew or make Elizabeth cross.

So a few minutes later, Andrew and Emily Michelle and I went into our front garden.

"Keep Emily away from the road," Elizabeth called after us.

"We will," I promised. Then I turned to Emily and looked into her dark eyes. "Okay," I said, "today you're going to learn how to play a new game. It's called It."

"Da?" said Emily, pointing to something across the garden.

I looked at Andrew. He shrugged.

"Emily, pay attention," I said. "Now

Andrew is going to be It, and he's supposed to run after us. He's supposed to try to catch one of us. Ready? Here we go."

I ran round the front garden. Andrew ran after me. Emily watched us and laughed.

I stopped. "Emily's not doing anything," I said.

Andrew didn't care. He crashed into me. "Got you! You're It!" he cried.

"That's not fair!" I cried. "I stopped because Emily's not playing."

Andrew was about to argue with me when I noticed something across the road. Hannie was wheeling her bike out of her garage. She hopped on to it, sped down her front drive, lost control, bumped over the kerb, and fell on to the road.

"Oh, no!" I shouted, just as Hannie wailed, "Ow, ow, ow! Help me!"

I forgot that Hannie and I were angry with each other. I ran to the pavement. Luckily, no cars were coming, so I dashed across the road. I helped to move Hannie and her bicycle on to the Papadakises' front

78

lawn. Then I helped Hannie inside to her mother.

Hannie's mouth was bleeding all over the place. She spat two teeth into her hand.

"Oh, Mummy!" sobbed Hannie. "*Look!*"

"It's all right," said Mrs Papadakis calmly. She told Hannie to rinse her mouth out at the kitchen sink. "They were baby teeth and they were loose anyway."

"I know," said Hannie. But she couldn't stop crying.

Her mother gave her a hug. She washed Hannie's face. Hannie was still crying.

"Does your mouth hurt a lot?" asked Mrs Papadakis.

"No," replied Hannie. "Not much. But now I'm too ugly to marry Scott."

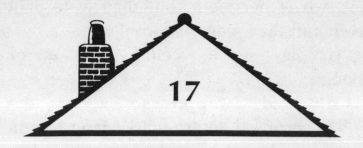

Scott and Hannie

After Hannie had stopped crying I went back to my house. I was sorry Hannie had hurt herself, and I was sorry she thought she was ugly. But I didn't want to stay with her. Hannie had been unkind to me for almost two weeks. She hadn't said, "I'm sorry," to me. She hadn't even thanked me for helping her when she fell off her bike.

Daddy didn't know about that, though. And the first thing he said when I came back from the Papadakises' was, "How's Hannie? Andrew told me about her accident."

"She's all right," I replied. "She knocked out two of her teeth, but they were baby teeth and they were already loose."

"Hannie must be feeling pretty awful, though."

I shrugged. "I suppose so."

"I'm surprised you're not keeping Hannie company. You two are always together. Well, you can visit her after lunch," said Daddy.

"Do I have to?" I asked.

"Don't you want to?"

"I suppose so," I answered. I didn't feel like telling Daddy about our fight.

So after lunch I had to go back to Hannie's house.

I was quite relieved when Scott Hsu arrived at Hannie's at the same time as I did! Now I wouldn't have to face Hannie by myself.

"Hello, Scott," I said.

"Hello, Karen," he announced. He rang the doorbell.

Linny let us inside. "Hannie's up in her room," he said.

Scott ran up the stairs to Hannie's bedroom. I followed slowly. What was I supposed to say to Hannie? Sorry you've knocked your teeth out — now you look as ugly as I do? Sorry you've been a pain in the neck? Sorry Gloriana is a rotten haircutter?

At least I was still looking pretty good. When I got dressed that morning, I hadn't put on hair ribbons or jewellery or anything. I'd just brushed my hair and I looked . . . nice.

Scott had reached Hannie's room. I was trailing behind him, but I could hear him say, "Karen's here too."

I took a deep breath and went into Hannie's room. She was lying on her bed, reading a book. She looked sad.

"I heard about your accident," Scott told Hannie. (I didn't say anything. I just stood in the doorway.)

"Did you?" said Hannie in a small voice.

Scott nodded. "Andrew Brewer told me." (Had he told the whole world?) "Well, I was just wondering," Scott went on. "Will you feel well enough to have the wedding tomorrow?"

Hannie shook her head. "You don't want to marry me now," she said. "Look at me." She opened her mouth and showed Scott the two gaps where her teeth had been.

"So what?" said Scott.

"I'm not perfect. I'm *ugly!*" cried Hannie.

Scott's eyes widened. "I don't care what you look like," he said. "I'm not marrying your *face*. I'm marrying *you*. Okay?"

"Okay," said Hannie. She smiled a tiny smile.

Scott left then. As he ran down the hall, he called over his shoulder, "See you tomorrow at our wedding!"

I put my hands on my hips and stared at Hannie. She wouldn't look at me.

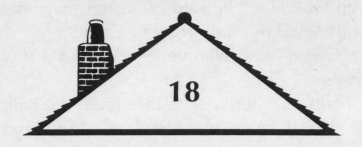

"I'm Sorry, Chandrelle"

As Hannie wouldn't look at me or even say anything, at last *I* said, "My father made me come over here. I didn't want to, but he said I had to."

Hannie glanced up. "I suppose if I were you, I wouldn't have wanted to come here either."

"You've been really unkind to me," I told her.

Hannie nodded. "I can't believe how nice Scott was to me. I'm sorry I've been unkind, Chandrelle."

"It's Chantal," I replied. (Wouldn't anybody *ever* get my name right?)

"Chantal," Hannie repeated. She paused. "Do you know what I've been thinking ever since I fell off my bike?"

"What?" I said. I sat on the edge of Hannie's bed.

"I've been thinking," Hannie began, "that you must have been feeling awful for the last few weeks. It's terrible to think you look ugly. It's even worse to think people won't like you because of that."

"It *was* awful," I said. "It was awful when I looked in the mirror, and it was awful when the boys called me the Bride of Frankenstein. But you know what was the worst thing of all?"

"What?" asked Hannie.

"When you told me I couldn't be in your wedding because I wasn't perfect."

Hannie lowered her eyes. "I know that wasn't fair. I'm not sure why I did that. I suppose I just wanted the wedding to be . . . perfect. But I've been thinking this morning

and I'm really glad you came because now I can tell you what I've decided. Just because I didn't like your teeth and hair it didn't mean I couldn't like you. Remember what Scott said? He said, 'I'm not marrying your *face*. I'm marrying *you*.' That's the same thing. Anyway, I suppose nobody's perfect."

"That's what Daddy always says," I told Hannie. I smiled at her.

"I know," she replied. "My parents say the same thing."

"Do you think it's true?" I asked.

"What? That nobody's perfect?" said Hannie.

"Yes."

Hannie looked thoughtful. "Yes," she said finally. "I do think that's true, Chantal. . . . Hey! I got your name right!"

I giggled. "You can call me Karen now."

"Can I? Why?"

"Because I don't think I need fancy things any more. I'm not wearing my hair ribbons or my jewellery. See? And you just said you like me even if I'm not perfect. So I don't have to be glamorous either. I can just be Karen Brewer again."

"Good," said Hannie. "I like Karen Brewer better than Chantal and Tiffanie and all those other names. Um, do you still want to be in my wedding?"

"Of course I do!"

"Oh, great! Gosh, we'll have to decide what you're going to wear."

"How about my pink party dress?" I said. "And my party shoes."

"Perfect. You can put flowers in your hair, just like me. Gosh, I'd better remember to pick them."

"What else have you got to do?" I asked.

"Oh, lots of things."

For almost an hour, Hannie and I sat in her room. We talked about her wedding.

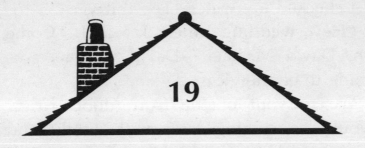

Hannie's Wedding

The next day was wedding day! That morning I didn't lie around in my bed, I jumped out! The wedding was going to be at eleven o'clock, and I had to be ready. First I ate breakfast. Usually I get dressed first, but I didn't want to spill orange juice or cereal on my party dress.

As soon as breakfast was over I put on my pink dress, my white socks with the rosebuds on them, and my party shoes. I brushed my hair. Then I looked at myself in the long mirror in Daddy and Elizabeth's room. I decided I looked almost . . . pretty.

I checked my watch. Ten-thirty.

"Hey, wedding time!" I yelled. "Come on, David Michael." David Michael was going to be the vicar.

We ran out of the front door. Kristy would be coming later with Emily and Andrew. They would be wedding guests.

When we reached the Papadakises' garden, David Michael and I found Hannie and Linny (who was going to be the best man) and Sari. Sari's Hannie's little sister. She's Emily's age. She was going to be the flower girl.

Hannie looked ever so pretty. She was wearing high-heeled shoes and her mother's wedding dress. She had to hold the dress up high so that she wouldn't trip over the hem, but that was all right.

Sari looked pretty too, but I knew she had no idea what was going on. And Linny and David Michael looked handsome in their suits. They looked cross, though. That was because they hate wearing suits.

"Hello, Karen!" called Hannie when she saw me. "Come here! I've got our flowers!"

Hannie had picked dandelions. She poked them into our hair. I hoped they wouldn't fall out.

"Where's Scott?" I asked.

"He's . . ." said Hannie slowly, looking around, "right there!" Walking proudly into the Papadakises' yard were Scott and his older brother. They were both wearing suits, only they didn't look cross. Scott was grinning.

"Is everyone here?" I asked.

"Everyone except the guests," Hannie replied.

The guests arrived in twos and threes — Kristy, Andrew, Emily, Nancy, some children from down the road, Scott's parents, and Hannie's parents.

Hannie's mother was carrying a camera. She was the wedding photographer.

When everyone had arrived, Hannie said, "Let's get started. Sari, throw your flower petals. Daddy, the music."

Sari was holding a basket full of bits of tissue paper. She flung the whole basket on to the ground. Everyone laughed. Sari cried and her father had to pick her up. But first he turned on a tape recorder. Hannie wanted to get married to the tape of "Take Me Out to the Ball Game". It's her favourite song.

Scott and Hannie stood in front of David Michael, the vicar. Linny and I stood just behind them. I wasn't sure what the bridesmaid and the best man were supposed to do.

"Okay," said David Michael. "Um, let's see. We are gathered here today for this wedding. This wedding of Hannie and Scott."

Click, went Mrs Papadakis's camera.

"Hannie, do you take Scott to be your husband?" asked David Michael.

"I do," said Hannie seriously.

"Scott, do you take Hannie to be your wife?"

"I do," said Scott. Then he whispered loudly, "Linny, we need the rings."

Linny hadn't been paying attention. He jumped a mile. Then he put his hand in his pocket and pulled out two of my dentist rings. I'd lent them to Hannie the day before.

Scott took the rings. He gave one to Hannie. She slipped it on to Scott's finger, and Scott slipped the other ring on to Hannie's finger.

"Okay!" cried David Michael. "You two are married! You can kiss."

"No way!" shrieked Scott and Hannie at the same time.

Click, click, click went the camera.

All the guests cheered.

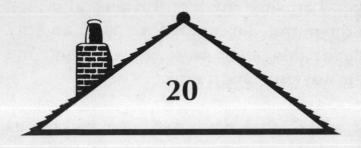

A Wedding for Karen?

On Monday morning I woke up in my bed at Mummy's. I was feeling happy, even though I was sorry my weekend at Daddy's was over. I was sorry the wedding was over, too. That had been fun.

But I was happy to be plain old Karen Brewer again. I didn't need sparkly nail varnish. I didn't need Mummy's make-up. I didn't need necklaces and the ankle bracelet or my hair ribbons. I didn't even need a new name.

I got dressed quickly. Dressing went much

faster when I only had to put on clothes. Then I brushed my hair. I looked at myself in the mirror. I examined my teeth and my haircut. My teeth were growing and my hair was growing. Perfect.

At school that day, two amazing things happened.

The first one happened after Seth had dropped me off at school and I was walking to the front door. I passed those two big fifth-grade girls who had smiled at me, and guess what? (You won't believe this.) They'd had their hair cut just like mine! Honestly!

I ran to Miss Colman's room.

"Hannie! Nancy!" I cried. (Miss Colman wasn't there yet, so nobody reminded me to use my indoor voice.)

"What? What is it?" exclaimed my friends.

"Those two big girls, the ones I told you about on Friday —"

"The ones who smiled at you?" interrupted Nancy.

"Yes," I replied. "Well, they've got haircuts like mine! I've just seen them."

Nancy's eyes grew wide. So did Hannie's.

"You — you've started something the big girls have copied," said Hannie in awe. "Gosh!"

The second amazing thing happened in the playground that day. Our class was crowded around Hannie. Everyone wanted to know about her wedding.

"Are you *really* married?" asked Natalie.

"Well . . . no," replied Hannie. "David Michael isn't a real vicar, but Scott and I can pretend. He's my best boyfriend."

"Did you get any wedding presents?" asked Jannie.

"No, but I've got a wedding ring." Hannie held her hand out. On it was the dentist ring. It was gold with a red jewel. I'd decided to let Scott and Hannie keep the rings.

"My bridesmaid," Hannie went on, "was Karen. She was dressed up. She looked very beautiful."

"Thank you," I said. "Hannie looked beautiful too. She was wearing her mother's *real* wedding dress."

"Oooh!" said all the children.

"My mother took photos at the wedding," said Hannie. "I'll bring them to school when they've been developed."

Just then I felt someone tug at my arm. I turned around. Yicky Ricky was behind me.

"Hey, Chantal," he whispered. "Come here." He pulled me away from the crowd. "Chantal," he said again, "I was wondering. One day, would you think about marrying me? Maybe?"

Ricky wanted to marry *me*?

I looked at him. I could tell he was serious. He was even a little nervous.

Still, I almost said, "No." After all, this was Yicky Ricky, who used to call me horrible names and throw spitballs at me. But then I remembered he was the only one who'd remembered my glamorous names.

So I smiled at Ricky Torres. "Yes," I told him.

Ricky grinned back. "Thanks," he said. "Thanks, Chantal."

"It's Karen," I told him. "It's just Karen Brewer."

GREEN WATCH by Anthony Masters

GREEN WATCH is a new series of fast moving environmental thrillers, in which a group of young people battle against the odds to save the natural world from ruthless exploitation. All titles are printed on recycled paper.

BATTLE FOR THE BADGERS
Tim's been sent to stay with his weird Uncle Seb and his two kids, Flower and Brian, who run Green Watch – an environmental pressure group. At first Tim thinks they're a bunch of cranks – but soon he finds himself battling to save badgers from extermination . . .

SAD SONG OF THE WHALE
Tim leaps at the chance to join Green Watch on an anti-whaling expedition. But soon, he and the other members of Green Watch, find themselves shipwrecked and fighting for their lives . . .

DOLPHIN'S REVENGE
The members of Green Watch are convinced that Sam Jefferson is mistreating his dolphins – but how can they prove it? Not only that, but they must save Loner, a wild dolphin, from captivity . . .

MONSTERS ON THE BEACH
The Green Watch team is called to investigate a suspected radiation leak. Teddy McCormack claims to have seen mutated crabs and sea-plants, but there's no proof, and Green Watch don't know whether he's crazy or there's been a cover-up . . .

GORILLA MOUNTAIN
Tim, Brian and Flower fly to Africa to meet the Bests, who are protecting gorillas from poachers. But they are ambushed and Alison Best is kidnapped. It is up to them to rescue her *and* save the gorillas . . .

SPIRIT OF THE CONDOR
Green Watch has gone to California on a surfing holiday – but not for long! Someone is trying to kill the Californian Condor, the bird cherished by an Indian tribe – the Daiku – without which the tribe will die. Green Watch must struggle to save both the Condor and the Daiku . . .

THE BABYSITTERS CLUB

Need a babysitter? Then call the Babysitters Club. Kristy Thomas and her friends are all experienced sitters. They can tackle any job from rampaging toddlers to a pandemonium of pets. To find out all about them, read on!

Look out for:

You'll find these and many more fun Hippo books at your local bookseller, or you can order them direct. Just send off to Customer Services, Hippo Books, Westfield Road, Southam, Leamington Spa, Warwickshire CV33 0JH, not forgetting to enclose a cheque or postal order for the price of the book(s) plus 30p per book for postage and packing.